W9-CUP-812

Lily's Garden

DEBORAH KOGAN RAY

ROARING BROOK PRESS

BROOKFIELD, CONNECTICUT

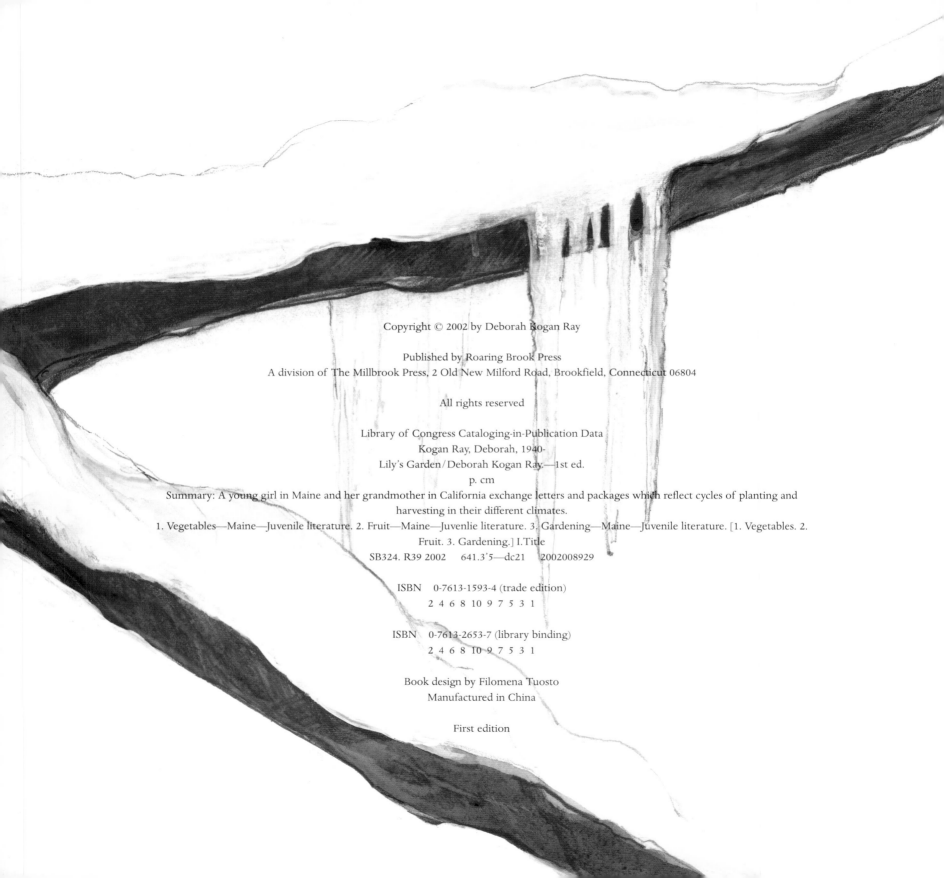

Published by Roaring Brook Press
A division of The Millbrook Press, 2 Old New Milford Road, Brookfield, Connecticut 06804

Library of Congress Cataloging-in-Publication Data
Kogan Ray, Deborah, 1940-
Lily's Garden/Deborah Kogan Ray.—1st ed.
p. cm
Summary: A young girl in Maine and her grandmother in California exchange letters and packages which reflect cycles of planting and
harvesting in their different climates.
1. Vegetables—Maine—Juvenile literature. 2. Fruit—Maine—Juvenlie literature. 3. Gardening—Maine—Juvenile literature. [1. Vegetables. 2.
Fruit. 3. Gardening.] I.Title
SB324. R39 2002   641.3'5—dc21   2002008929

ISBN   0-7613-1593-4 (trade edition)
2 4 6 8 10 9 7 5 3 1

ISBN   0-7613-2653-7 (library binding)
2 4 6 8 10 9 7 5 3 1

Book design by Filomena Tuosto
Manufactured in China

First edition

For Isabel and Lily, my models

This morning, a box of juicy oranges arrived from Grandma and Grandpa.
They've left their house, that's up the road from ours, to live in California.
It will be a whole year until I see them again.

ORANGES are a citrus fruit.
They originated in India and
have been grown for more
than 4,000 years.

Columbus brought orange seeds to America
from Spain in 1493.

The first California orange groves were planted
in the 1700s by Spanish missionaries.

Until a hundred years ago oranges were
considered rare and were eaten only as a treat
on holidays.

Growers plant different varieties of oranges in
their groves so that mature fruit is available all
year. It takes two to four years for an orange
tree to bear fruit.

Valencia oranges are the most commonly grown.
Blood oranges are red.
Navel oranges have no seeds.
Mandarin oranges are small.
Sour oranges are
used to make
marmalade.

"It's strange to be in a place that stays warm all the time," Grandma's note said. "All the flowers are blooming and the citrus groves are full of fruit. There's an orange tree by our kitchen door. Every morning, I snip a ripe orange for my breakfast. Lily, can you imagine picking fruit in the middle of winter?"

I can't.

Here in Maine, our apple trees are bare. All our fields are hidden under a blanket of snow.

Grandpa calls this quiet time.
Nothing is growing.

JANUARY

HOW TO MAKE MAPLE SYRUP

You'll need a large shallow pan or a washtub, a hot fire (an outdoor brick barbecue works well for a fireplace), and a grownup to help you. Pour the sap that you collected into your container and set it over the fire. Then you have to stir and stir until the water from the sap boils away and it thickens into syrup. When the syrup is ready, spoon it through a cloth filter and pour it into clean glass storage jars.

MAPLE LEAF CANDY

Ask a grownup to help you make maple candy. Boil 2 cups of maple syrup until it is frothy. Stir until it looks milky. Pour into maple leaf molds. Remove from molds when cool. Makes 1 lb. of candy.

Our stream is running with melting snow. The icicles are dripping faster. Grandpa says these are the clues that tell you it's sugar weather.

Today, Daddy and I climbed up the hill to where the big maples grow. We went from tree to tree, drilling holes three inches deep. Then we lightly tapped spouts into each hole and hung gallon milk jugs from each spout to collect the sap. Until the sugar run is over, in about six weeks, we'll check our taps every couple of days. We'll collect the sap that has dripped into the jugs, then boil it down to make maple syrup.

It takes forty gallons of sap to make one gallon of maple syrup!

I promised to send a jar to Grandma and Grandpa as soon as it is ready.

"I can't wait. You know how much I love hot maple syrup on Grandma's special blueberry pancakes," Grandpa said.

FEBRUARY

VEGETABLES GROWING IN CALIFORNIA

Artichokes

Garlic

Beans

Lettuce

Broccoli

Radishes

Carrots

Squash

Eggplant

Tomatoes

HOW TO START SEEDS INSIDE

Fill cardboard pots with a mixture of vermiculite
and potting soil.
Put one seed in each pot.
Label the plant trays and put them in a sunny
window.
Water every day.
Depending on what you planted, seedlings will
emerge in about two weeks.

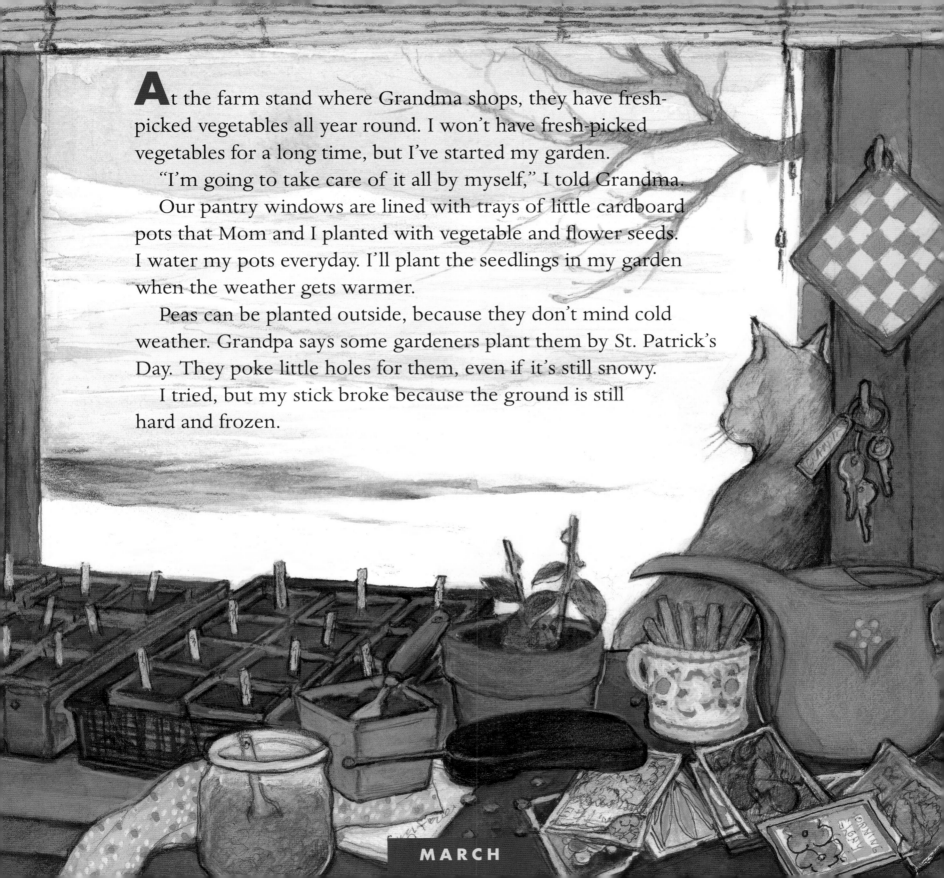

At the farm stand where Grandma shops, they have fresh-picked vegetables all year round. I won't have fresh-picked vegetables for a long time, but I've started my garden.

"I'm going to take care of it all by myself," I told Grandma.

Our pantry windows are lined with trays of little cardboard pots that Mom and I planted with vegetable and flower seeds. I water my pots everyday. I'll plant the seedlings in my garden when the weather gets warmer.

Peas can be planted outside, because they don't mind cold weather. Grandpa says some gardeners plant them by St. Patrick's Day. They poke little holes for them, even if it's still snowy.

I tried, but my stick broke because the ground is still hard and frozen.

MARCH

LILY'S GARDEN SET:

Trowel

Fork

Spade

DAFFODILS are sometimes
called narcissus or jonquils.
They can be grown indoors in
winter by rooting the bulbs on
a dish of small stones. Bulbs
bloom year after year when planted outdoors.

Other spring flowers that grow from
bulbs: crocus, hyacinth, tulips.

Last fall, Grandma and I planted a big bed of daffodil bulbs. We dug the bulbs in one by one and covered them with leaves for a blanket.

Grandma said, "They will be one of the first spring flowers."

When I called Grandma and Grandpa to thank them for my birthday present, I told them I had cut a bunch of daffodils for my party table. My present was a set of garden tools and little wooden sign that says "Lily's Garden."

"I've turned the soil in my garden. I'm ready to plant," I said.

APRIL

VEGETABLES LILY
HAS PLANTED IN HER GARDEN

Bush beans

Peas

Cabbage

Peppers

Carrots

Pumpkins

Chives

Tomatoes

Cucumbers

Zucchini

Eggplant

Lettuce

The maple trees have new green leaves. There are blossoms on our apple trees. Grandpa calls this wakeup time. Everything is growing.

My pea vines are climbing up their trellis and the baby lettuces are getting rounder. The chives are budding.

"I put in my six tomato plants today," I told Grandma.

She said, "Don't forget to put buckets over them at night. They'll need caps to keep them warm. It can still get frosty."

MAY

WHAT LILY IS DOING IN HER GARDEN

Her vegetables are growing.

She's harvesting peas.

She's planting a new lettuce crop,

and sunflowers,

and marigolds.

She's weeding.

Bees are pollinating.

Moles are making holes.

Groundhogs are burrowing.

This morning, when I went to pick peas, a family of rabbits hopped out of my garden. Then I saw what they had done.

The bunnies ate all my lettuce!

"I always loved bunnies. Now, I know why Grandpa sometimes calls them pesky critters," I told Grandma

Grandma laughed. "Lily, you're growing their favorite food. That's why they come to nibble. Ask Mom to put camphor balls around your garden. The smell makes bunnies stay away. They don't like it."

I don't, either. But I did ask Mom to do it.

I'll plant seeds for a new crop of lettuce tomorrow.

JUNE

WATERMELONS originated in the Kalahari Desert in Africa.

The first recorded watermelon harvest was 5,000 years ago in Egypt. It is shown in hieroglyphics on the walls of ancient buildings.

African slaves brought watermelons seeds to the United States. George Washington and Thomas Jefferson grew watermelons in their gardens. There are 200 varieties of watermelon grown in the U.S.A. They are grown year round in warm areas.

For a watermelon vine to bear fruit, it needs honey bees to pollinate the flowers.

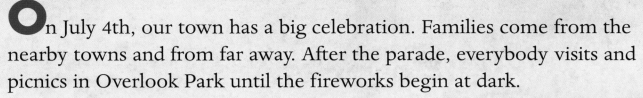

On July 4th, our town has a big celebration. Families come from the nearby towns and from far away. After the parade, everybody visits and picnics in Overlook Park until the fireworks begin at dark.

Mom made hamburgers for our picnic. I mixed the potato salad and sprinkled it with chives that I snipped from my garden. Daddy bought a great big watermelon at the supermarket for dessert.

Grandma bought a fresh-picked watermelon at her favorite farm stand for their picnic.

"We've invited a few friends for a cookout. But I wish I was going to the parade and watching the fireworks with you," she said.

I wish Grandma and Grandpa were here, too.

JULY

LOWBUSH WILD BLUEBERRIES
thrive in the northern climate of
the coastal fields and barrens
of Maine. They have grown in
North America for 13,000 years.

GRANDMA'S BLUEBERRY PANCAKES
Makes twelve 4-inch pancakes

1 cup milk
1 large egg
¼ cup sour cream
1 cup flour
1 tablespoon
  baking powder

1 tablespoon sugar
¼ teaspoon salt
2 tablespoons melted butter
½ cup fresh Maine
  blueberries, washed and
  picked over

In a large bowl, stir milk, egg, and sour cream
together. In a separate bowl, stir together flour,
baking powder, sugar, and salt. Add flour mixture
to milk mixture. Stir batter until large lumps
disappear. Stir in melted butter. Add blueberries,
gently folding them into batter.

For each pancake, ladle
two large tablespoonfuls
of batter onto a hot,
lightly oiled griddle and
cook for 2 to 3 minutes
per side. Serve with
maple syrup.

There are signs all over town that say "Rakers Wanted." The big blueberry farms are ready to bring in the harvest.

When it's blueberry time, Mom and I go picking every day in our fields. She rakes. I pick mine by hand.

Mom laughs. "Lily, you'll never fill your pail, if you keep snacking on them that way."

This morning, we used Grandma's recipe to make blueberry pancakes for breakfast.

"I poured lots of hot maple syrup on my pancakes, just like Grandpa does," I told Grandma.

TOMATOES are a fruit. They originated in Mexico and South America. Early explorers brought them to Europe in the 1500s. They called them "love apples."

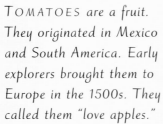

ZUCCHINI BREAD
Makes 2 loaves

3 eggs
1½ cups sugar
1 cup vegetable oil
2 medium zucchini,
    peeled and grated
1 tablespoon vanilla

3 cups flour
1 teaspoon salt
1 teaspoon baking soda
1 tablespoon cinnamon
1 cup chopped walnuts

Beat eggs in a large mixing bowl; add sugar, oil, zucchini and vanilla. Sift together the flour, salt, baking soda, and cinnamon, then add walnuts and add to the egg and zucchini mixture. Pour into two buttered and floured loaf pans and bake at 350 degrees for one hour.

My tomato plants are sagging with tomatoes. I've had to put in more stakes to hold them up. Every day, Mom and I fill baskets with the big red tomatoes, cucumbers, peppers, carrots, and bush beans that we've picked from our gardens. There are heads of lettuce, cabbages, eggplants, and huge zucchini squash, too.

Mom and I are busy jarring tomato sauce for winter. We've made lots of zucchini bread, too.

Today, I set up a table down at the end of our road, to sell some of my vegetables.

"I made a sign that says Lily's Farmstand," I told Grandma.

Lily's Farmstand

AUGUST

APPLES are a member of the rose family. They originated in China. In North America, the first apple trees were planted by the Pilgrims. In colonial times apples were called winter banana or melt-in-the-mouth.

George Washington's favorite hobby was pruning his apple trees.

Apple trees take four to five years to produce their first fruit.
Some apple trees will grow to be over forty feet high and live for over a hundred years.
Apples can be grown farther north than most other fruits. They grow in all fifty states.

The oldest apple variety is the "Lady Apple."
The most popular variety is the "Delicious Apple."
McIntosh apples are grown in Maine.

Our blueberry fields are autumn red. Leaves are turning color on the maple trees. Summer's over and it's time for apple picking.

Daddy sets up the ladders. Mom and I get the canvas bags from the shed. We each put one on. She makes sure mine is fastened tight.

"Up we go, Lily," Daddy says.

When I'm up in the tree, I lean against the ladder for balance. You need to twist hard to snap the apple stems off the branches. When my bag is full, I climb down and empty it into a bushel basket. Then I climb back up into the apple tree and pick some more.

"We've picked bushels and bushels of apples," I told Grandma.

SEPTEMBER

Native Americans used pumpkin as a staple in their diets for thousands of years. They introduced them to the Pilgrims. Just like today, early settlers used pumpkins in a wide variety of recipes from soups to pies.

PUMPKINS are gourds. They are the same family as squash and zucchini.

Jack-o-lanterns weren't always carved from pumpkins. They began hundreds of years ago in Ireland when faces were carved in turnips.

ROASTED
PUMPKIN SEEDS

2 cups pumpkin seeds
2 tablespoons vegetable oil
1 teaspoon salt

Scoop seeds from the pumpkin. Rinse off strings and pulp. Mix seeds with oil and salt in a bowl. Spread seeds on a baking sheet in a single layer. Bake at 350 degrees for 15 minutes, until crisp and golden.

All of my pumpkins have been cut from the vines. Daddy and I carved some of them into Halloween jack-o-lanterns.

Today, my class had Pumpkin Day, when we weigh and measure. Mom had to drive me to school because my pumpkin was too big and heavy for me to bring on the bus. Lots of other kids brought big pumpkins, too.

"Mine was the biggest!" I told Grandma and Grandpa. "And I grew it all by myself."

OCTOBER

ABOUT HARVEST CELEBRATIONS

There is an annual celebration at the completion of the harvest in every society that grows food.

In the U.S.A., Thanksgiving celebrates the Pilgrim's first harvest in 1621. Native Americans were holding harvest celebrations long before the Pilgrims came. Some tribes still hold an annual Green Corn Ceremony, when the first sweet corn is ready to harvest.

In ancient Eygpt, harvest festivals honored the god Min, who they believed made the soil rich for growing things.

For thousands of years, Jewish people have celebrated "Sukkoth" to remember when they lived in makeshift shelters during harvest.

In Ghana, a yam festival called "To Hoot at Famine" is celebrated.

The garden is finished. Daddy and I covered it with a blanket of seaweed we brought up from the beach. Our pumpkins, squash, and apples have been stored in the basement. The pantry shelves are lined with jars of tomato sauce. The freezer is filled with bags of peas, beans, and blueberries.

Mom and I have labeled envelopes of vegetable and flower seeds that we saved from the garden. We will plant them next spring.

I told Grandma, "I picked the seeds from the heads of the sunflowers that I grew. I'll fill the birdfeeders with them when it's snowy."

"Those hungry birds will be glad you shared your harvest," she said.

NOVEMBER

Decorating an evergreen tree is an old German tradition. In the 1800s, the tradition of a Christmas tree spread to England when Queen Victoria married a German prince, Albert. German immigrants who settled in Pennsylvania brought the tradition to America.

Christmas trees are grown on tree farms and plantations. They are grown in all fifty states (including Hawaii).

Arizona cypress grows in the southwest.

White pine grows in the north and Canada. It is the state tree in Maine.

Colorado blue spruce grows in the northeast.

Frazier fir grows in the southeast.

We are almost ready for Christmas. I've bought presents for everyone with the money I earned at my farmstand. Mom and I baked Christmas cookies.

Today, we drove up the snowy logging path to the Christmas tree farm. It took a long time to find the perfect tree.

"Stand out of the way, Lily," Daddy said, before he sawed it.

"This will be the best Christmas ever," I told Daddy and Mom.

Grandpa and Grandma are coming home tomorrow.

DECEMBER

Mom will carefully unwrap the paper snowflakes and glittery glass balls. Daddy will string the twinkling lights. Grandma and I will make cranberry ropes and twine them around our Christmas tree. Grandpa will lift me way in the air to put the star on top.

This year, it will be harder for him because I've grown so much.